Torn

By

Denise Hill

ACKNOWLEGMENT

I want to thank God for allowing me to write my fifth book. I want to thank my family and friends for their continued support and encouragement. I encourage everyone to step out of their comfort zone and do whatever it is that you have always dreamed of doing because you only live once and never live with having any regrets.

I can truly say that I am blessed and I want to thank God for all the great opportunities that have come my way and the ones that are on the way. How many people can say that they are doing everything their heart desires, well, I can truly say I'm doing it from hosting a radio show, hosting and producing a women's and men's talk show, filming, writing, screenwriting, leading a film networking group, acting, producing and directing and, being the president of MEA Midwest Entertainment Associaton and not to mention owning a record label called Throwback Records.

DH Publishing Company
Indianapolis, IN 46250

TORN

Cover Design: DH Publishing Company
ISBN: 978-0-692-14912-6
Editor: DH Publishing Company
Email address: dhpublishingco@gmail.com
Website: www.dhpublishingco.com

PROLOGUE

Parked down the street in a rental car, Perry and two of friends watched as Kenneth pulled off.

"Follow that motherfucker," Perry yelled! "Today is not your lucky day. I told you payback would be a bitch. Today you will feel my wrath."

Perry's adrenaline was running high.

"I can't wait to beat his ass."

Perry's friend laughed.

"Man, I can't believe you let this white dude take your girl and beat that ass," Michael Bell said.

His friends burst out laughing. Perry rolled his eyes.

"Fuck yaw niggas!"

When Kenneth's car came to a stop at a red light. Perry jumped out of the car and ran up to the driver's side of Kenneth's car. Perry jerked open the driver's door and pulled Kenneth out with the help of his friends. They threw Kenneth into the back of the trunk of the rental car where he would be taken to an abandoned building.

CHAPTER ONE

Denise Caldwell could no longer hide behind the fake smiles pretending to be happy until the day when she met the sexy, successful, Criminal Attorney Kenneth A James. Since then, it had turned her entire world upside down. The Chemistry between the two was off the chain, but there was just one minor problem and his name was Perry Rogers. Perry had been Denise's live-in boyfriend for the past three years. As far as Denise knows, They had dissolved their relationship. She just wished Perry would realize it and move on, but what Denise didn't know was that Perry had his own suspicions about her seeing someone else.

Perry noticed how Kenneth always looked at Denise whenever he would pick her up and how he always waited for her until he arrived. He had questioned her about Kenneth frequently, but Denise would always tell him they were just friends, but after today's conversation with Kenneth, his suspicions were right.

Denise had no idea what was in store for her this evening.

It was a warm late October afternoon. The wind was blowing a warm breeze, and the sun was shining brightly as the pedestrians made their way to their destination. The traffic backed up a mile away on Pennsylvania street as Denise stood outside the Chase bank waiting for her ride. Denise paced back and forth, cursing Perry under her breath. Denise agreed to let Perry use her car this morning against her better judgment to go on some job interviews, but now she regrets it. Denise checked her watch for the fifth time, and still, Perry was nowhere in sight.

"I can't believe he is late again. This will be the last time I let him take my car," She said as she made her way across the street to catch the city bus to make it home before it got dark. The last thing she wanted was to be downtown after dark.

Denise stood patiently waiting for the bus, trying to keep her eyes straight ahead and not on the idiot standing next to her. This was one of the many reasons she didn't enjoy catching the bus. You had to deal with all the cra-cra's and the fact that the buses were never on time.

Denise continued to stand quietly waiting, and just as she looked up, he sees the number 19 turn the corner, but just then she heard someone calling her name.

"Denise, Denise over here," Perry yelled out as he waved her over. "Thank God!"

Denise made her way back across the street in front of her workplace where Perry parked.

"What took you so long," Denise yelled as she approached the car. She could smell marijuana and as she moved closer to the car. She could tell he had been drinking.

"Perry, what did I tell you about smoking that shit in my car and driving while you have been drinking?"

"Girl shut the fuck up. You better be glad I picked your stupid ass up."

"What! The last time I checked this was my car. And you better be glad I let your stupid ass drive my car without a license."

Out of nowhere, Perry's fist collided with Denise's jaw, causing her face to hit the side of the window.

"And you better tell that boyfriend of yours to stop calling my house or there will be some trouble."

Denise looked over at Perry. Guilt written all over her face.

"Perry, what are you talking about?" Denise asked as she held her hand to her face.

"Do I look stupid to you Denise, huh? You know damn well what I am talking about. I am talking about that attorney friend of yours. I know you two are fucking."

The ride home was quiet. Denise could tell something was up with Perry and as they turned the corner of her apartment complex, her heart dropped to her stomach. She now regrets not letting Kenneth get her away from this situation.

Kenneth was a close friend of Denise at first. He had an office in the Same building where she worked. She met Kenneth several months ago and explained her situation to him about Perry. Kenneth cared for Denise and wanted to take her away from her situation. Denise was a little leery of Kenneth's intentions in the beginning, but as they became closer, she slowly fell in love with him. The only problem was that she didn't know how to get rid of Perry. She could have called the cops and had him removed, but that would have caused more problems that she didn't want.

After having a conversation with Perry today, Kenneth decided that today was the day that he would get Denise out of her situation before something bad happened to her.

Kenneth and his business partner Scott Studdard, an African American male in his early forty's arrived at Denise's and waited outside in his car for her arrival home. By looking at the two today, you would never guess they were high power attorneys. They looked more like thugs.

Just as Kenneth was about to call Denise, he sees her vehicle pulling into her assigned parking spot.

"There she goes." Kenneth pointed to her car.

"Man, why are we doing this? Why are we acting looks thugs and not attorneys? You know this could blow up in our face. Man, we could lose everything if this goes bad. Is she worth it?"

"Yes, she is worth it," Kenneth said as he looked over at Scott.

Denise had no idea that her life was about to change forever. Denise hesitated to get out of the car. Perry got out and looked back at Denise, who was still sitting inside the car.

"You better hurry your ass up."

Kenneth and Scott sat in the car and watched as Perry and Denise walked upstairs to her apartment. Perry unlocked the door and walked in. Denise slowly made her way to stand in front of the door and as soon as Denise stepped foot inside her apartment, Perry grabbed a hold of her and slammed her to the ground. He climbed on top of her and straddled her as he started beating her with his fist. Denise screamed out for help.

Kenneth and Scott watched as Perry pulled Denise inside, and then they heard her cry for help. Kenneth and Scott rushed upstairs to the second floor to her rescue.

Kenneth was the first one inside the apartment and when he saw her on the floor, he went off as she was laying there, blood gushing out of her mouth and nose while Perry was on top of her beating her senseless. Denise tried to protect herself from the blows with her hands, but Perry's punches were much too powerful, Perry knocked Denise unconscious.

Pulling out his 45, he pointed the gun at the side of Perry's head. Perry stopped and looked up at Kenneth, whose gun was now directly in his face.

"Get your ass off of her," Kenneth growled.

Perry slowly got up and stood to face Kenneth.

"Take Denise to the car," Kenneth yelled to Scott.

Scott bent down and picked Denise up and carried her out the door.

"Now it's just you and me mother fucker. Now, what was that shit you were talking about over the phone earlier?" Kenneth struck Perry in the face with the butt of his gun.

"Cat got your tongue now," Kenneth struck him again.

"I am taking Denise with me and when I come back for her belongings, I better not see your ass anywhere in sight and if I do, I will definitely make your bitch ass disappear."

CHAPTER TWO

Denise wrote in her diary

For the most part, my life is slowly taking a turn for the best. It took two weeks to recover from Perry's beating. A beating I will never forget, but I am safe from harm and with the man I have grown to love. I would have never imagined myself falling in love with a white man, but I love him to death and that's all that matters. Each day that goes by, the love that I feel for Kenneth gets stronger, but the fear of running into Perry remains on my mind. I hate to think about this, but I feel as though something is lurking around the corner and will show its ugly self and destroy what we are trying to build together. Some days this feeling keeps me from being happy. I try hard to think positive and put my trust in God, but some days are harder than others and sometimes I can't shake this awful feeling.

Denise continued to sit in bed thinking about things and then at that moment, she decided she would no longer allow negative thoughts to keep from being happy with the man she loved. Denise closed her journal, got out of bed, and hid her journal underneath the mattress.
Denise walked downstairs to the kitchen. She stood in the entryway admiring the sexiest butt cheeks on a man that she had ever seen. Denise eased up behind him and grabbed a hold of his ass.
   "Good morning sexy," She whispered in his ear.
   "Good morning, Dee. Did you sleep well?"
Kenneth turned around to face her and pulled her close to him and kissed her. She couldn't tell Kenneth that she had not had a good night's sleep since she moved in, so she lied.
   "I slept like a baby."
   "That's good to hear. I've been a little worried about you seeing how much you toss and turn in your sleep at night."
Kenneth looked her dead in her eyes, with his eyebrows slightly arched and with a serious demeanor, tried to see if there was any truth in what she was saying.

"Why are you looking at me like that?"

"Denise, would you ever lie to me?" Denise hesitated before answering.

"Of course not."

"Um… Okay, why don't you have a seat and let me fix you my famous pancakes for breakfast."
Kenneth wasn't sure she was being honest with him, but right now he would let it slide.

"Um… everything smells so good and like always, I am starving."
She took a bite of the pancakes, and they seemed to melt in her mouth.

"These pancakes are delicious. Where did you learn to cook?"
Kenneth laughed as he joined her at the kitchen table.

"My family owns a restaurant in Gatlinburg, Tennessee, and every summer as an adolescent, my cousins and I had to work there and learn the family business from cooking to keeping the books. We worked there until we graduated from college. Now every year around Thanksgiving, we all go back down there for about two weeks and work in the restaurant."

"Oh, that sounds like fun."

"It's a lot of fun. The entire family looks forward to this every year. You should think about coming with me this year."

"I don't know about that. How would your family feel about you bringing a black woman?"

"They wouldn't have a problem with it. You're not the first black woman that I have been in a relationship with."

"Oh, I forgot, Mr. I love black women," they both laughed.
Denise inhaled her breakfast, while Kenneth sat and watched the woman who had stolen his heart.
Denise looked up at Kenneth and smiled. "What are your plans for today?"

"I have a few errands to run, other than that, nothing. Is there something you want to do?"
Denise smiled slyly. "I would like to spend the day laying in bed with you watching movies and other things."

She got up from the kitchen table, walked over to Kenneth who was still sitting, wrapped her arms around his neck and kissed him on the cheek.

"Oh, would you now," Kenneth said as he pulled her onto his lap.

"Why don't I pick up some movies on my way back?" He said in between kisses.

"Sounds good to me. And for dinner, we can order in," Denise said as she looked up at Kenneth, admiring his blue eyes.

Kenneth pulled Denise's face closer to his. He outlined her lips with his tongue before devouring her mouth as his hands made their way down to her rear end.

"Um… you know I love how that ass feels."

"I know something else that you like the feel of," Denise laughed as she pulled away from Kenneth.

"Oh, no you don't," Kenneth said as he pulled her back to him.

"You know I am so happy that you moved in here with me."

"Did I really have a choice in the matter after your phone conversation with Perry?"

"Yeah, you did. You could have gone back to him, but you know once I put the D down you couldn't resist me."

"Whatever," Denise swatted at Kenneth.

An hour later, Denise was busy in the kitchen when Kenneth walked in.

"I'm heading out. It should only take an hour. Don't miss me too much."

Denise turned to face Kenny, "You just make sure you hurry on back because I have someone who is dying to connect with you."

"You don't have to tell me twice," Kenneth said as he kissed Denise on the lips.

Parked down the street in a rental car, Perry and two friends watched as Kenneth pulled off.

"Follow that motherfucker," Perry yelled! "Today is not your lucky day. I told you payback would be a bitch. Today you will feel my wrath."

Perry's adrenaline was running high.

"I can't wait to beat his ass."

Perry's friend laughed.

"Man, I can't believe you let this white dude take your girl and beat that ass," Michael Bell said.

His friends burst out laughing. Perry rolled his eyes.

"Fuck yaw niggas!"

When Kenneth's car came to a stop at a red light. Perry jumped out of the car and ran up to the driver's side of Kenneth's car. Perry jerked open the driver's door and pulled Kenneth out with the help of his friends. They threw Kenneth into the back of the trunk of the rental car where he was taken to an abandoned building.

Two weeks earlier

Kenneth, Scott and another friend name KJ Dullen helped Denise move her belongings out of her apartment and into storage.

In the meantime, Perry was over at a female who lived in the same apartment complex and watched as they moved Denise. When they left, Perry used the females car to follow them to the storage unit and later to Kenneth's place.

Perry removed Kenneth from the trunk. They took him inside the abandoned warehouse. They placed Kenneth in a chair with his hands tied behind his back.

"See motherfucker payback is a bitch."

Perry looked around the warehouse for an object. He found what looked like a crowbar and struck Kenneth in the temple with it repeatedly. His friends threw punches, hitting him in the face and chest. They continued to beat Kenneth until he was no longer breathing. Once the three men realized what they have just done, they panicked.

"Perry man, this was not part of the plan. I cannot go to jail for murder," Jomo Cole said as he started pacing back and forth.

"I know man, we fucked this up," Michael Bell said.

"Shut your fucking mouth and let me think," Perry yelled! He paced back and forth until he came up with an idea, "I got it. Help me get him in the trunk. I know the perfect place to dump his ass. It will be days before anyone discovers his body."

As the men put his body in the trunk, his wallet and phone fell to the ground.

CHAPTER THREE

Driving for miles, the men came to a deserted area. They got out and headed to the back of the car. Perry looked around before opening the trunk and removing the body.

"We can dump the body in the woods up ahead."
Moving quickly, the men moved deeper into the woods carrying the body when they came upon something that looked like a ditch large enough to hide a body.

"Let's dump him here and cover his body with those leaves and branches over there."
The men dumped the body and buried it under some leaves and tree branches, and once they covered the body, they made their way back to the rental.

"Now if we all keep our mouths shut, no one will ever suspect us," Perry said as he lit a cigarette.

"How can you be so sure that no one saw you when you dragged him from his car? You were in such a damn hurry to get at him you did not stop to think about anyone who would see you," Michael pointed out.

"Did you think about anyone who would see you before you hopped your happy ass out of the car to help me? We cannot change what has happened, but I swear if any of you motherfuckers snitch on me, I will make sure we all go down for this," Perry said, making it clear to them they were all just as guilty as he was.

Denise looked at the clock again. It had been four hours since Kenneth left. He was not answering his phone and his business partner was concerned since Kenneth had not dropped off the documents needed for their client's court hearing on Monday.
As Denise paced back and forth, she stopped when she heard a knock at the front door. She ran to answer it in hopes of it being Kenneth

but when she opened the door, she came face to face with two white male police officers.

"Are you Mr. James' housekeeper?" The first officer asked.
Denise looked at the officers sideways, "No, I am Denise Caldwell, Mr. James' girlfriend," She said with a slight attitude.

"Is Mr. James home?" The second officer asked.

"No, he is not here. I have been expecting him for hours now. Is there something wrong, officer?"

"We found his car abandoned at a stoplight, but he was nowhere in sight," the first officer said.

"Oh, my God! Where did you find his car?"

"His car was not too far from here. We found it at the corner of Sergeant and Fall Creek," the second officer said.
Denise escorted the two officers to the living room. She dropped into the nearest chair and grabbed her chest.

"Kenneth left out four hours ago. He is not answering his phone, and he did not drop off some documents to his business partner."

"What type of work does he do?"

"He's a criminal attorney."

"I see. How can we get in contact with his business partner?"
Denise went into the study and grabbed one of Kenneth's business cards from his desk and jotted down Scott's number on the back of it. She walked back into the living and handed it to the officer.

"Should I come down to the station and file a missing person report?"

"I would give it a few hours and then if he still hasn't returned I would come down, but let's hope it doesn't come to that."
Denise walked out with the officers and stood on the porch looking up and down the street.

"Kenneth, where are you!" Denise asked.

Later that evening and still no word from Kenneth, Denise called Scott to find out if he had heard anything from Kenneth.
Denise went into the living room and picked up her cell to call Scott.

Scott was in his living room watching a football game when his cell rang.

"Denise, I am sorry, but I have not heard from Kenneth. It doesn't look good, especially since they found his car abandoned. This sounds like there is some foul play involved."

"Scott, I am about to lose my mind. This cannot be happening to me. I would swear on a stack of bibles that Perry has something to do with this."

"Did you tell this to the police?"

"No, not yet. I will if I have to file a missing person report or if they find his blood in the car. They towed his car to dust for fingerprints and to see if there are any traces of blood in the car."

"You should have told them. Just keep your fingers crossed that he shows up. And call me as soon as he does, or if you hear anything from the police. Oh, and call me if you need anything or just want to talk."

"I will. I will let you know if I hear anything. Thanks, Scott."
Denise walked outside onto the patio. She looked up at the moon as if she was looking for some answers. The wind blew gently against her skin, causing chills to run down her spine. The thought of never seeing Kenneth again was too much for her to think about, but deep down inside, she knew she would never see him again. She knew something bad had happened, and she knew who was to blame.

Four months and still no word from Kenneth or any news from the police. They could not find any fingerprints other than Kenneth's in the car, and there were no traces of blood. She told the police what she thought happened, but the police could not locate Perry.
The little bun that was growing in her stomach was getting stronger each day. Scott had been wonderful. He made sure she wanted for nothing. He had been by her side since the day she found out she was pregnant with Kenneth's baby.
After weeks of debating with Scott, he talked Denise into quitting her job at Anthem and joining the firm as his executive secretary. At first, she wasn't so sure this was the right move, but after a few weeks, this

turned out to be the best decision for her because of her pregnancy. Scott allowed her to work from home three days a week. This was a blessing. Scott had been so good to her. He had even started going to her doctor's appointments.

Today, Denise was having an ultrasound, and Scott was right by her side.

"Oh, my God! I can't believe I'm having a boy, Scott. And listen to his heartbeat." Denise was so excited.

Scott laughed, "I hear it, Denise."

"Kenneth would be so happy."

"He would be more than happy."

Denise held back the tears that had threatened to fall.

Afterward, Scott and Denise had dinner at the District Tap restaurant on 86th Street.

"Man, this steak is so delicious," Denise said in between bites.

"I can tell," Scott said as he watched her eat.

Scott chuckled, and then out of nowhere, Denise broke down crying. She tried to hold the tears back that was threatening to fall, but she couldn't. She was carrying a man's baby who just up and disappeared without a trace.

"Denise, baby, what's wrong?"

Denise wiped her face with the napkin

"I'm sorry Scott, but it's so hard. I try to pretend that I'm strong and that I am moving on with my life, but every time I think about the baby, I have thoughts of Kenneth. I miss him so much."

"I know Denise, it's understandable."

Scott put his hand on top of her hand.

CHAPTER FOUR

"**Well**, it looks like your John Doe has come out of his coma," Tequila said as she passed Gladys in the hall.

"Are you serious?" Gladys asked with excitement.

"That woman is so man crazy it's pathetic," Tequila Sims said. Gladys walked into the hospital room where John Doe was laying in bed. Gladys pulled up a chair and as usual, she sat and talked to John Doe about her day.

"I heard that you have come out of your coma?" Gladys waited, but there was no response from John

"Come on, John, talk to me." John opened his eyes and stared at Gladys.

"Oh my, you have the prettiest green eyes that I have ever seen," Gladys said. John continued to stare at Gladys as if she were a Creature from the Black Lagoon as she continued to talk.

"Do you ever shut up?" Gladys looked up and laughed, "Oh, so you can speak. Well, it is about time because I am tired of doing all the talking.'

"Where am I? The last nurse wouldn't answer me," John Doe asked as he tried to get up.

"Be still. You are at Mercy Hospital. John, please hold still John, let me page your doctor."

"What am I doing here and how long have I been here?"

"Let me get your doctor, he will explain everything to you, just hold still," Gladys said as she walked over to the phone and phoned the nurse's station. "Yes, this is Gladys and I would like to have doctor Corey Garrad paged and sent to room 113 ASAP. Thanks." It took the doctor some time to get through to John, but now he knew how he ended up there at Mercy. He remembered nothing he didn't know if he had a wife or if he had any children. He couldn't remember a damn thing to save his life. John continued to wonder why someone would beat him so badly to where he almost died

Four months earlier

Henry and his friends were out in the woods deer hunting when Henry tripped and fell face down onto something. As he landed on it, they heard a sound that sounded like a moan.

"What the fuck," Henry screamed!
Henry and his friends began moving the leaves and branches to discover a body. The man's eyes looked at Henry and his friends as they stood frightened.
Henry pulled out his phone and called his neighbor, who was the sheriff.
The sheriff arrived in no time with three of his deputies. They had John escorted to Mercy Hospital in Cincinnati and John had been there since. John had no identification on him, so they called him John Doe.

"This is so fucking crazy that I can't remember anything."

"It happens a lot when there's trauma to the head. It will take some time John before your memory comes back, but in the meantime, let's try to get you walking and eating on your own again," Gladys said as she smiled at John.
Gladys had been working with John for about two weeks. He could now feed and bath himself and walk without a walker. They will boot John from the hospital in another week.

"John, have you given any thought to what we talked about as far as where you will go once it's time for you to check out of here?" Gladys asked as she stood looking at how sexy John looked.

"No, I haven't."

"You have seven days to figure something out or you will be out on the street."
Gladys was about to make her rounds around the hospital

"Where am I going to go? I don't know anyone, I have no money. How can the hospital just kick me out in my condition?" He said, frustrated and angry. "I know I had a life before this. Has anyone reported me missing?" He continued to ponder over his existence.
Gladys shrugged her shoulders as she left out of his room. She felt sorry for him so that's why she invited him to stay with her until his

memory came back and besides, who wouldn't want a sexy hunk like John in the next room.

The next morning, John waited for Gladys. He knew he had to do something or he would be homeless.

Gladys entered John's room, "Good morning sunshine."

"Good morning, Gladys. I need to talk to you about your offer. I thought about what you said and since I have nowhere else to go, I guess I will have to take you up on your offer."

"Oh, so you're coming home with me?"

"Must you make it sound so sleazy?"

"Well, Just so you know, I am not trying to get you home so I can do you. I am not desperate by a long shot. I get plenty of male attention, probably more than I care to."

"Oh, I wouldn't doubt that."

John thought about what Gladys had said. She was a very attractive and youthful woman with her green eyes, perky breasts, her round behind, and legs for days. Then he thought about it. She had seen him naked while he was in a coma. Now he felt violated. He laughed to himself.

John watched as she checked his vital signs. He noticed a dimple in her right cheek. He noticed how her lip turned up and how her eyes glistened when she smiled. The more he noticed about her, the more intrigued he became.

Denise's and Scott's first argument and it had something to do with Kenneth's disappearance. For the love of her, she could not understand why Scott's attitude was so fucked up when it came to Kenneth now. Scott's attitude was so bad that she had to distance herself from him on a personal level. It appeared as though Scott's only concern was replacing Kenneth in her bed, which would not to happen.

Over the months, she had grown to care a lot about Scott like a big brother, but romantically, she was not feeling him and wished he would understand. Four months had gone by and now Denise was feeling the pressure from Scott to take their relationship to another level.

"Denise, why can't you see that I care about you and that I want to be there for you and little Kenneth."

"Scott, I understand that, but I don't feel the same way. I love you like a brother, not a lover. I want you to be here for Kenneth. I want you to be the uncle he doesn't have. You were Kenneth's best friend and partner, doesn't that mean anything to you?"

Kenneth shook his head, "What can I do to make you change your mind?"

Denise walked over to stand in front of Scott.

"Nothing Scott, I will never feel the way you want me to feel. Like I said, I look at you like a brother."

"Okay, I guess I will have to accept that. Let me let you finish doing what you were doing. If you need anything, just call me," Scott said as he walked toward the front door with his tail between his legs.

CHAPTER FIVE

Twenty minutes later, Denise was sitting in the living room watching TV when she heard a knock at the front door. She wobbled to the door, thinking it was Scott. Scott had left his briefcase, so she called to tell him. When Denise opened the door, she got the surprise of her life. There stood the last person she would ever want to see.

"What are you doing here?

"What do you mean what am I doing here? I heard you were expecting, and I wanted to know if the baby is mine?"
Perry pushed his way inside.

"No, Perry, stop! I would never have a child with you."
Denise slapped Perry in the face. Perry got aggressive.
Scott pulled up in front of the home and sees a man trying to push his way into the home. Scott jumped out of his car and ran up the walkway.

"You better let me in this bitch!"
He pushed Denise down and stepped inside and stood over her.

"You are a sick, pathetic fuck. I would never bring a child into this world with you."
Perry grabbed her up by the throat until she was standing. He raised his right hand to strike her.

"How many times have I told you about that damn mouth of yours? That mouth will always get you an ass whipping," He said as he struck Denise in the face again.
Scott ran and grabbed Perry from behind. Scott put Perry in a choke hold and dragged him outside onto the porch and slammed him to the ground. Scott reached for his gun and pulled it out. He slapped Perry in the face with it and then pointed the gun at him.

"What man puts his hands on a woman, especially a pregnant one? Get up and if I ever see you around here again, you will be one sorry son of a bitch!"

Perry got up. He walked slowly to his car. He got in and sat for a minute before taking off. Perry pulled off and drove slowly past the condo, looking at Scott as he stood.

"It isn't over, you bitch ass nigga," Perry yelled. Scott held up his gun and pointed at Perry, "I think it is," Scott yelled back.
Scott stood as he waited for Perry to leave before heading inside the home.
Denise was in the living room sitting when Scott walked over to Denise.

"Are you okay?" Scott asked as he lifted Denise's chin up to get a better look at her.

"Yes, Scott, I'm all right. A little shaken up, but I'm fine."
Scott hesitated, "well, Denise, I don't think it's safe for you to stay here alone. I can stay here with you, or you can come to my place."
Denise thought about what Scott said. She knew Scott was right, but she didn't want him getting the wrong idea about them.

"Scott, you're right. Why don't I fix up the guest room for you?"

They released John Doe from the hospital at noon. He hung around the hospitals waiting area waiting for Gladys to get off work at 2. He read two magazines, watched a little tv and walked around the hospital until 2.
An hour later, Gladys pulled into her driveway and cut the engine,

"Well, here we are. Home sweet home."
Gladys opened her door and go out. John continued to sit.

"Are you just going to sit there?" Gladys asked as she looked back at John.
John looked over at her and laughed. He opened the car door and got out. He looked at the little brick ranch home. He wondered what type of home he had.
Inside, Gladys led John down the narrow hallway to a room at the end of the hallway.

"Here you go. It's nothing fancy or anything, but it beats sleeping outside."

"It's not bad at all and yes, anything beats sleeping outside. Thank you so much!"

"Don't worry about it. Make yourself at home. I will get dinner started. Join me in the kitchen when you're ready."

John sat down on the bed and stared into space, trying to get his thoughts together. He wanted more than anything to remember. He wondered how many kids he had if he had any. He wondered if he had a wife or if he was dating someone. He had so many questions, but no answers to any of them.

After an hour later, John made his way into the kitchen just as Gladys was taking out a pan of garlic bread.

"Um… something smells good."

"Thanks. Here, taste this for me and tell me what you think."

Gladys handed John the wooden spoon to taste her homemade spaghetti sauce.

"Good. Just the right amount of oregano. Dang, how would I know that am I a cook?"

Just then, John started thinking about a recipe for homemade spaghetti sauce and all the ingredients, and then he remembered working in a restaurant. John stood there in a daze as Gladys called out to him.

"John, John, John."

"I'm sorry, were you saying something?"

Gladys had a worried look on her face.

"Is something wrong, John?"

"Oh no, I was just thinking about something."

"Well, you better take a seat and eat before your food gets cold."

John looked down at the table and sees that Gladys had already fixed his plate. He walked over to the table and took a seat and was ready to dig in.

CHAPTER SIX

Five months later, Denise was in the delivery room. Denise shed tears as she watched the nurse take her baby away to clean him up.

"You did it, baby girl," Scott said with the biggest smile plastered on his face.

The nurse walked over to Denise, "So, what's his name?"

"Kenneth James Jr.," Denise said between sniffles. It broke her heart to know that baby Kenneth would never know his father.

"He's gorgeous with his green eyes."

Denise smiled as she thought about Kenneth.

"He looks just like his daddy."

The nurse looked at Scott and then back at Denise, "I think he looks more like you," The nurse said.

Two days later, Denise and little Kenneth arrived home. Scott was being very helpful and was very protective of little Kenneth.

"When your family gets here make sure they use the gloves and masks when handling the baby." Scott held up a box of gloves and masks.

Denise laughed and shook her head.

Two weeks later

Gladys was sitting in the living room watching television while John sat at the desk with the laptop when he came across a court case. He was so intrigued by this particular case. He continued to read when out of nowhere his memory came back little by little.

"Oh, my God!"

John stood as he remembered having a law firm with Scott as his business partner, he remembered the hijacking and assault and he remembered Denise and all of his feelings for her overwhelmed him. He was so confused right now because he had fallen in love with Gladys. A memory of John and Denise making love in the bedroom flashed through his head. John staggered back a little as he grabbed his chest.

"Damn, what am I going to do?"

Gladys looked up, "John, are you okay?"

John stood still for a moment and then he looked over at her, "yeah, I'm good."

Later that night, John lay awake in bed with Gladys as she cuddled up next to him. He was not in the mood to be intimate with her, so he turned his back to her.

Gladys raised up, "John, what's wrong?"

"I just have a lot on my mind right now."

"Do you want to talk about it?"

"No, go to sleep, sweetheart."

John tossed and turned all night. He couldn't get Denise out of his head. He wondered what she had been doing and if she had moved on with her life. It broke his heart to know that he had been gone for this long, leaving her hanging wondering what had happened.

The next morning, John and Gladys were sitting at the kitchen table as usual on an early Saturday morning.

"Whatever is on your mind must be really something. You tossed and turned all night long," Gladys spoke as she eyed John.

"Sorry," John said as he avoided eye contact with her.

"Don't be sorry, just talk to me, John," Gladys pleaded.

John hesitated. He didn't know if he should tell her about his memory coming back or not. Then he decided that she had been too good to him to keep any secrets from her.

"I have something to tell you," John said.

Gladys had a frightened look on her face. John laughed as he looked at her.

"Relax, it's nothing bad. My name is Kenneth James," he said, smiling.

"Oh, my God! You got your memory back. So your Kenneth James."

"Yes, I'm an attorney from Indianapolis. I have a law firm with my business partner, Scott Studdard. It's called the Law firm of James and Studdard."

"I am so happy for you, Kenneth." Gladys got up from the table and walked over to him and hugged him tightly, and then she looked at him. She knew there was more, and she also knew there may be some things she didn't want to know right now. Kenneth stood up and pulled her to him.

"There's more. I have a girl back home. Her name is Denise."
Gladys pulled away from him, "I figured as much."
Kenneth pulled her back to him, "Gladys, that doesn't take away from what I feel for you. I'm just a little confused right now. I have never been in a situation like this before. I need some time to rethink things over," Kenneth said as he held Gladys in his arms.

"Sure, Kenneth, take all the time you need," Gladys leaned her head up against Kenneth's chest.

"I need a favor though. I need to use your car so I can go back to Indiana. I want to go to my Condo, contact my partner Scott, and I need to see Denise. I need to explain the situation to her. I want her to know that I just didn't disappear on her and last, I need to take care of the people that did this to me."

"Sure, can I go with you?"

"I would rather go alone."

"Okay, but I don't think it's a good idea for you to go after those guys. I think it would be best to go to the police and let them handle it."

"Yeah, right."

"Kenneth, can I ask you a question and I want you to be honest with me."

"What it is?"

"Where is this going to leave us?"
Kenneth didn't want to lie to her, but he didn't want to hurt her either. He knew his heart was with Denise, but he had to make sure she hadn't moved on with someone else first.

"Gladys, I can't make you any promises right now. I know this is not what you want to hear, but it's the God's honest truth. I can't say where this will leave us. I will probably go back to Indiana since I have my business there if it still exists."

"I understand," Gladys got up from the table and walked out. Kenneth continued to sit, feeling like the bearer of bad news.

Gladys walked back in with car keys in hand.

"Do whatever you need to do, Kenneth," she kissed him on the forehead and walked away.

Kenneth hopped on the interstate and drove 4 miles before taking exit I-74W. He wondered how Denise would react when she sees him. He was so nervous because he had no idea if she had moved on with someone else or if she was still living in his condo. He knew nothing.

Two hours later, Kenneth turned onto the street he lived on for many years. The street looked a lot smaller to him, but as he continued to drive, he realized nothing had changed. Kenneth continued driving until he came to his condo and to his surprise, he sees his Jag sitting out front.

"What the fuck!" Kenneth said as he pulled in behind his car. He was so confused. He saw Denise's car, so he was wondering if someone had been driving his car. Kenneth sat for a few minutes before getting out.

When he got out of the car, he looked around the neighborhood and at the houses. He turned back around and decided he must do what he came to do. He slowly made his way up the walkway. His heart pounded as he got closer to the front door. Once he reached the door, his hand rose slowly to knock. He knocked once, twice and three times before the front door opened and when it opened, he got a surprise. A shirtless man stood at his front door. What the hell, he thought before he recognized the man standing at his front door. They both stood there in silence, glancing at one another.

"Oh, my God! Is this who I think it is?"

Kenneth continued to stand in silence wondering why his business partner and best friend was in his home shirtless.

"What's going on Scott and why are you here?"

"Oh, oh, it's not what you think," Scott stuttered.

"No, it's what I see," Kenneth said as he pushed his way into his condo.

"Where's Denise?"

Just then Denise walked in with baby Kenneth. "Oh my God!" Denise staggered back against the wall

"Kenneth, is that you?"

Scott grabbed a hold of baby Kenneth and walked into the living room, leaving the two to talk. Denise grabbed her chest as tears formed in her eyes.

"Kenneth, where have you been and what happened to you? Why did you just up and disappear?"

"What is Scott doing in my home, Denise? What is going on between you two?" Kenneth stood looking directly at Denise, waiting for her response.

"Kenneth, it's not what you think."

"Well, what is it then? What should I think? I have been missing in action for a little over nine months and then when I resurface you and my best friend is in my home together and he's shirtless. I don't know why I even came back. You know what, you have two months to pack your shit up and leave my home."

"Kenneth, what's wrong with you? Come and sit down and let me explain everything to you, please! There's nothing going on between us. We're just friends, I promise." Denise tried to hug Kenneth, but he pushed her away.

"Just friends, I doubt that. There's nothing to explain Denise, I have seen what I needed to see." Kenneth takes one more look at Denise before heading out the door and does an about-face.

"You know, I loved you and I still do, but you and my best friend. How could you do this to me?"

"Kenneth, listen, baby, you have it all wrong. I told you we are just friends. Scott was here to help me out when you just up and disappeared on me."

Denise followed behind Kenneth as he walked out the door. She followed him down the walkway to the sidewalk. She reached for his arm, but he jerked away. She stood there as he got into his car. She banged on the passenger window.

"Kenneth, please hear me out!"

Kenneth never looked her way as he pulled off, leaving Denise standing there crying.

Kenneth drove around until he found a place to park. He pulled into a Kroger parking lot, cut the engine and sat there. The tears he fought so hard to keep from coming slowly rolled down his face. He knew he was taking a chance that Denise could have moved on with someone else, but he never thought it would be with his best friend. As Kenneth thought about the scene, the baby flashed in his mind. Whose baby was that, he wondered.

Twenty Minutes later, Kenneth hopped on the interstate heading East back to Gladys.

CHAPTER SEVEN

Denise walked back inside as her heart broke for the second time. She paced back and forth in the living room, trying to figure out what she could do to get Kenneth to listen to her.

"How could he just leave us?" How could he?"

"Denise, calm down."

"Calm down, how can I calm down? Why didn't you say something? Why didn't you tell him it wasn't what he thought?"

"I tried to tell him," Scott pleaded.

"Well, you didn't try hard enough."

"He will be back."

"He wants me out of his home in two months. Where am I going to go?"

"Now you know that's a stupid question. My home is your home whenever it needs to be."

"Scott, I appreciate that. I appreciate all that you've done, but that's definitely not going to get me Kenneth back by doing that and you know that. You know what, I am not going anywhere until he hears me out!" Denise continued to pace back and forth.

"Denise, can you check to see if my shirt is dry." Scott looked down at baby Kenneth as he rocked him.

"How could you do Uncle Scott like that? Not only did you spit your milk up on me, but you peed on me."
Scott laughed as he continued to rock Kj to sleep.

Kenneth walked in five hours later, and as he walked through the door, Gladys could tell something was wrong. Gladys walked up to Kenneth and wrapped her arms around him.

"Hey babe, how did it go?"
She could tell that he had been drinking. Kenneth took a step back and ran his hand across his face.

"Not good babe. I found my best friend and business partner at my condo shirtless."

"What!"

"Yes, he had the nerve to answer the door when I knocked."

"Well, what did you say?"

"I asked him what was he doing there? And he said it's not what you think. Everyone's favorite line once they get caught."

"So what did you catch him doing?"

Kenneth looked at Gladys sideways as he walked further into the living room and took a seat on the sofa. Gladys followed him and sat down right next to him and grabbed a hold of his hand.

"I mean, you said he had his shirt off, but there could have been several reasons he was shirtless. Did you let him explain?"

Kenneth looked at Gladys again.

"Who side are you on?"

"You know I am on your side, but sometimes things look one way, but when you found out the truth, it's different from what you thought."

Kenneth sat back on the sofa and lay his head back with his eyes closed.

"I was so angry that I wouldn't have heard anything, even if I would have allowed them to explain the situation to me."

"Kenneth, that is not fair. What if the shoe was on the other foot, like in our situation in the very beginning? What if Denise came here to find you living with me and she didn't let you explain your situation to her? How would you feel? I'm just saying, babe."

Kenneth sat up straight and exhaled loudly, "I guess you're right."

Kenneth pats his lap for Gladys to sit on.

"You know, that's why I have fallen in love you." The words escaped his mouth before he knew it.

"You what!"

"Yes, I said it. I have fallen in love with you."

"So what about Denise?"

Kenneth hesitated before answering, "to be honest with you, when I laid eyes on her today the love that I felt for her came rushing in like a tornado, but to know she's with my best friend I can't get past that."

"But what if she's not with your best friend, how will you feel about her then? What I need to know is where will this leave us?"

"Truthfully, I can't say." Just then he remembered the baby. "Oh, I almost forgot, she had a newborn baby in her arms."

"A newborn?"

"Yes."

Gladys thought. A newborn and Kenneth had been missing for nine and a half months.

"How long had you two been sleeping with each other before you assault?"

Kenneth looked at Gladys with a puzzled look.

"Why do you ask?"

"Could the baby be yours?"

"I never thought about that. It could be my baby, but why didn't she tell me?"

Because you didn't give her a chance to explain anything to you.

"Man," Kenneth lays his head back against the sofa.

"Monday morning, can you take me to get my car? I also need to go to the bank, but I don't have any ID. I need to make sure my bank accounts are still open, and to make sure my money is there. I also need to cancel my credit cards."

"Sure, just let me know what time, but Kenneth, you need to sit down and have a talk with Denise, if you like, I can be with you."

"I know, but I need to do this alone."

"Okay, but just make sure you let her explain everything to you."

Gladys walked down the hall to her bedroom.

Kenneth continued to sit on the sofa, thinking about Denise and the little baby he saw. He wondered if the baby was his.

"God, I hope so."

Gladys walked out of the bathroom from taking a shower to find Kenneth standing there.

"I want you," He walked over to Gladys and pulled her to him.

"Is it me you want or Denise?" She looked up at him and then pulled away from him. Kenneth took a step toward her and pulled her back to him. He bent his head down and forced his way into her mouth. He kissed her with so much intensity and all at once, he picked her up and carried her to the bed and lay her down softly. He removed the towel that covered her naked body. He undressed in front of her turning her on and when he was naked, he climbed between her legs and entered her with one quick movement. He raised her legs and placed them on his shoulder as he went deeper and deeper, faster and faster.

"Oh my God, Kenneth!" She screamed."

"Oh Denise, I love you!"

Denise awoke from a dream. She dreamed of Kenneth and her making love. She dreamed that Kenneth called out to her as he had done many times when they made love. She awakened and her nightshirt was drenched.

Back at Gladys's

"Who the fuck did you just call me? Get off of me!"

"Gladys, I'm so sorry."

Kenneth lay down beside Gladys. He tried to pull Gladys on top of him.

"Let me go!"

Kenneth raised up to sit on the side of the bed with his head down.

Gladys, please believe me when I say I am so sorry.

CHAPTER EIGHT

The next day, Gladys and Kenneth were heading for Indianapolis. They rode in silence the entire time. The only words that were exchange were when one of them asked or gave directions.

Two and a half hours later, Gladys pulled in behind Kenneth's car.

"Thank you," Kenneth said as he looked over at Gladys.

Gladys cut the engine, and the two just sat for a minute.

"Wait here," Kenneth said as he got out of the car

Kenneth walked up the walkway as Gladys sat in her car. Kenneth knocked on the door twice before Denise answered.

It surprised Denise to see Kenneth standing there.

"Can we talk?"

"Oh, so now you want to talk. Well, come on in."

Denise let Kenneth inside. She shut the door and walked behind him to the living room as she held baby Kenneth.

Kenneth looked around the condo. Nothing has changed.

"I left everything the way you had it."

"I appreciate that."

Kenneth tried to avoid looking at baby Kenneth for fearing of finding out that the baby belonged to Scott.

Denise could sense he avoided looking at the baby.

"Would you like to hold your son?"

Kenneth couldn't believe what he had just heard. My son?

"Yes, your son."

Denise pulled back the blanket so Kenneth could see his green eyes.

"Whose son did you think it was?"

Kenneth laughed as he looked into his son's eyes

He looked over at Denise, "I thought Scott was the father."

"Well, if you would have taken the time to look at the baby or ask you would have known that Scott could not have been the father. Two African American people cannot produce a mixed child."

39

"I'm sorry that I thought the worst. Can I ask you something and please be honest with me? Are you and Scott seeing each other?"
Denise laughed.

"No, we are not! Scott has been a godsend since you left. He was there for me during my entire pregnancy. He even hired me as his secretary at the firm so I could have flexible hours during the pregnancy. You owe him a lot."

Kenneth felt so small knowing that he had been sleeping and had fallen in love with Gladys. Come over here and sit so I can tell you what happened.

"Just a minute. I have a package for you."

Denise walked out of the living room and into the bedroom to grab the package. She walked back into the living room with the package in hand.

Denise handed the package to Kenneth.

This came about three months ago. I didn't even bother to open it.

Kenneth handed Denise the baby to open the package.

"Thank God!"

He opened the package to find his credit cards, wallet, bank card, car keys and cell phone.

"How did you get my car here?"

I had it towed from the police department after they finished dusting for fingerprints. Now, are you going to tell me what happened?

"Yes, have a seat."

Kenneth explained everything from the beginning to now. He told her about Gladys but left out the part about him fallen in love with her.

Denise thought about what Kenneth said and what he didn't say.

"So, do you love her, Kenneth?"

Kenneth couldn't look her in her eyes.

"Okay, I take that as a yes. So where does that leave the baby and me?"

"Denise, I will always be here for you and the baby no matter if we are together or not, I owe you that much."

"No, Kenneth, you don't owe me anything. All I ask is that you help take care of your baby. Oh, and we will be out of here in no time."

"Denise, you don't have to do that."
Kenneth grabbed a hold of her and tried to pull her to him.
Denise with tears in her eyes pulled away from him, but he pulled her back to him and kissed her.

"Kenneth, please don't."
Denise cried.

"Baby, don't cry. I love you, Denise, I never stopped loving you."

"How can you say that when you were with another woman?"

"That doesn't matter. Once I got my memory back, my feelings for you came back full force."

"So who is it going to be?"

"To be honest, I don't know right now. There's so much that I have to handle and think about, but whatever decision I make, just know I love you and probably will always love you and I will take care of my son. Can I hold him again?"
Kenneth reached down and picked him up from his bassinet.

"You know what, you have made me the happiest man right now."
Denise broke down crying.

"Baby, come here."
Kenneth walked toward Denise with the baby in his arms.

"No, Kenneth, I can't. You have no clue do, you. I have loved you, I have cried so many nights when you disappeared and now to find out you are alive and that you are in love with another woman, that just hurts me to the core. Please, just leave."

CHAPTER NINE

Gladys tires of waiting outside in the car, so she went to go inside to see what's going on. Gladys got out of the car, walked up the walkway to the front door. She stood there for a second, then she turned the doorknob and pushed the door open and stepped inside.

"I'm in love with you."

Gladys walked in just in time to hear Kenneth confess his love to Denise. Gladys coughed to get their attention as she moved further into the room. Denise was the first one to look at Gladys. Denise continued to stare at Gladys as she made her way to stand by Kenneth.

"Um… Is she the other woman?" Denise asked.

Denise looked at Kenneth and then back at Gladys. Gladys looked at Kenneth.

"Did you forget about me?"

Kenneth shook his head. "I'm so sorry."

Denise looked at Kenneth and rolled her eyes. She was so furious that he would bring his bitch to their home.

Gladys looked over at the baby, "Are you the baby's father?"

"Yes, he is!" Denise spoke.

"How sweet," Gladys said.

Gladys walked closer so she could get a better look at the baby.

"Aw, he's so gorgeous. Thank God he looks like his dad."

"Bitch, what is that supposed to mean?" Denise asked, standing with her hand on her hip.

"It means exactly what it means. You're a smart girl, you know exactly what I'm saying," Gladys stood looking directly at Denise.

"Stop it!" Denise, will you excuse me for a minute," Kenneth said, grabbing a hold of Gladys's arm and guiding her outside.

"What the hell is wrong with you? This is a side of you I've never seen, and it's a side of you I don't like."

"How could you impregnate someone like that?"

42

"What do you mean someone like that? Do you mean because she's black because my son is half black? You know, if you were a man, I would punch the shit out of you right now. What you need to do is to go back home, I can drive myself back, that's if I come back." Kenneth turned and walked up the walkway to the condo.

"Are you coming back, Kenneth?" Kenneth continued walking.
Gladys walked back to her car, opened the door, stopped and watched as Kenneth made his way into the home.
When Kenneth walked back in, he found Denise feeding Kenneth. He watched while she breastfed the baby.

"Damn!"
Denise looked up at Kenneth and rolled her eyes.
You know what you need to go on back to your fucking Barbie doll. I will be out of your condo shortly and you don't have to worry about the baby. Scott will step up to the plate.

"Oh, I see you got jokes."

"I can't believe you and then again, maybe I can."

"Denise, I'm sorry. If my memory hadn't left, this would never have happened."

"Right, blame it on your memory loss. Why the fuck didn't you wait until you got your memory back before getting with Ms. Barbie. What if you were married, what would you have done then?"
Denise took the baby and placed him on her shoulder to burp him.

"Can I do that?"
Denise ignored him.

"Denise, please don't shut me out. I want to be in his life and help with him."

"You shut yourself out when you hooked up with Barbie. I should be out of here by Friday."

"That's not fair, and I told you you don't have to leave."

"Life is not fair and besides, I can't stay here anymore, there's just too many memories, especially since I know you're alive now"
Denise lays the baby down in his bassinet. Kenneth walked up behind Denise and grabbed her.

"Man, it feels so good holding you."

"Well, don't get used to it," Denise said as she moved out of his embrace. There is no way I want you touching me after touching that bitch. Can you just leave so I can start packing?"

"Packing…, where are you going?"

"I don't know but I will be out of here soon, real soon."

Kenneth grabbed her and pulled her back to him.

"You don't have to leave, you can stay here as long as you want."

"Thank you, but no thanks."

Denise moved from Kenneth's embrace.

"Do nothing, Denise. Let me take care of some things and then we can sit down and talk."

"Talk about what Kenneth? You are in a relationship with someone, so there's nothing for us to talk about."

"Denise, please, just give me two days, okay."

Denise shook her head.

Kenneth walked over to the baby and picked him up. He kissed him softly on his cheek before leaving. He walked over to Denise and kissed her on the cheek.

"I'll be back in two days, I promise."

Denise watched as Kenneth walked out the door.

Kenneth pulled into the ATM drive through. He still remembered his pin number, now he just had to wait to see if his accounts were still active. Kenneth slid his card in, put in his pin# and chose which account he wanted to take money from. He pushed the button for $400 and waited to see what happened, and to his surprise, he heard the machine counting the money.

Kenneth grinned as he took his card and then his cash.

He pulled off in search of a hotel. He wanted a place where he could hide out until he put his plan into action to get Perry and the guys that almost killed him.

Kenneth took a right onto 82nd Street, going east until he came to the Shadeland exit. He took Shadeland until he arrived at a hotel called the Extended Stay. Kenneth checked into his hotel room. He paid for two nights, just long enough to do what he needed to do.

The next morning, Kenneth sat in his car parked in front of where Perry and Denise used to live. He had heard before they hijacked him that Perry was seeing a female that lived two doors down from where he and Denise used to live. He only hoped they were still seeing each other. Kenneth sat until 11:30 when was getting ready to leave to grab some lunch. As he started the car, someone pulled up in an old beat-up car. Kenneth glanced over and who did he see, it was Perry and some female. Kenneth stopped in his tracks. He cut the engine and sat back in his seat and pulled his hat down and grabbed a pair of sunglasses. He watched as the two got out of the car and walked into the apartment.

Kenneth got out of the car and walked around to the trunk. He opened the trunk and pulled his gun out and put it in the back of his pants. He shut the trunk, and that was when he noticed the female coming out of the apartment. Kenneth got back into his car and sat. He watched as the young lady got into her car and pulled away. He waited until the car was out of eyesight before getting back out. Kenneth jumped out of the car and quickly made his way up to the front door.

Kenneth Knocked twice before the door opened, and when Perry opened the door, Kenneth pushed him back and stepped inside and pointed the gun at Perry's face.

"Is there anyone else in this apartment?"

"No, it's just me."

Kenneth pulled off his hat, "Do you remember me?"

Perry had the look of horror on his face.

"Why don't you be a good little boy and have a seat over there?" Kenneth pointed to the chair at the kitchen table.

"Where are your boys?"

"What boys?"

"You know damn well what boys I'm talking about. Jomo Cole and Michael Bell."

Kenneth sees Perry's cell phone on the table and picked it up and handed it to him.

"Call your boy Jomo Cole and tell him to come over and say nothing stupid or that will be your ass."

Perry dialed Jomo's number

"Hey, Jomo I need for you to stop by, something has come up and why don't you bring Bertha with you." Kenneth yanked the phone from Perry and disconnected the call.

"Who the hell is Bertha?" Perry looked at Kenneth and smiled.
Kenneth waited for Jomo to arrive before calling Michael over. Kenneth wasn't taking any chances and tied Perry up. He pulled out some rope and masking tape from the inside of his jacket and tied Perry's hands and ankles to the chair, and then he put a piece of masking tape across his mouth. Once he finished, he heard a knock at the door.
It took Jomo twenty minutes to arrive. Jomo got out of the car with two other guys. They stood outside by the car talking before moving toward the apartment. Kenneth moved over to the door and unlocked it. He pulled it slightly open and hid behind the door.
Jomo walked in first and as he did, Kenneth yanked him inside and shut the door and locked it behind him.

"This has nothing to do with you guys unless you want to go down for attempted murder. I suggest you leave while you have the opportunity," Kenneth yelled out to the other two guys on the other side of the door. The two men thought about what Kenneth said and slowly back away from the door and head for the car. Kenneth guided Jomo to the second kitchen chair and tied him. He removed the tape from Perry's mouth.

"Now I need for you to call Michael Bell and if you try anything like the last time, I won't hesitate to put some lead in that ass."
Perry called Michael but got his voicemail, so he left a message for him to come over to the apartment ASAP.
An hour later, Michael pulled up, cut the engine and go out of the car. He walked toward the apartment. He had no idea what was in store for him. Michael walked up to the front door and before he could knock, the front door opened slightly. Michael pushed the door open further and walked in and when he did, he sees his partners tied up. Michael reached for his gun in the back of his pants, but Kenneth was standing right there. "I'll take that," Kenneth said as he grabbed the gun before Michael pulled it completely out.

"Have a seat over there and make yourself comfortable." Kenneth pointed to the empty chair at the table. He tied his hands and then his ankles.

"The next time you motherfuckers leave someone for dead, make sure he is dead.

CHAPTER TEN

Denise and her cousins were at the condo packing. Denise wanted to be out of the house before Kenneth came back because she knew if he returned today, she may have second thoughts about leaving.

"Are you sure you're making the right decision, Denise?" Pebbles asked.

"I don't know, but how can I compete with Blondie? I don't want to hurt anymore. What if I stay and he doesn't come back to me? Or what if he comes back and then decides he wants to leave and go back to Blondie, then I will still hurt either way?"

"Well, you're hurting now so what difference does it make? You're in love with Kenneth, so why are you doing this to yourself and the baby?" Jan asked.

"If he comes back to you, then you are the one he wants," Pebbles said.

"I'm sorry, but I can't take that chance."

Perry's apartment

"You know I thought long and hard about what I would do to you guys when I finally caught up to you, but since learning some things, I have spared your lives and let the judicial system deal with you. So you fool's, better thank my newborn son because if it wasn't for him, I would have tortured and killed your asses." Kenneth laid the gun down on the counter and reached into his jacket to pull out his cell phone and dialed 911.

"911, what's your emergency?"

"My name is Kenneth James, and they reported missing about 9 and a half months ago. They left for dead by three men that I have captured and have them at gunpoint, so I suggest you send some officers over here to handle the situation. I believe there were two officers that were working on my case name Nolen and Sparks."

"Well, it looks like I am finished here." Denise looked around the home and got a little emotional.

"Why, why did everything have to turn out this way?" Denise cried.

"Oh, honey, don't cry. Things will work out for the best, trust me," Pebbles said. Pebbles nodded to Jan.

As Pebbles continued to hug Denise, Jan made her way into the bedroom and pulled out an envelope from her purse and lay it on the dresser and then walked back into the living room.

"Well, if you guys are ready, I say let's blow this joint," Jan said.

Denise grabbed little Kenneth and wrapped him up and put him in his car seat. She walked to the front door stopped and looked back one last time.

"I will miss this place."

"No, you won't. It's time to make some fresh memories." Jan winked at Pebbles.

The two detectives arrived on the scene and approached the apartment with caution. Once they were inside, the detectives see the three men. One of them had been a suspect the entire time, they just couldn't locate him.

Kenneth spoke to the detectives for a while before heading back to his place.

Kenneth pulled up to his condo. He didn't see Denise's car and figured she was out running errands or something.

Kenneth walked in, and all at once, the emptiness hit him. He went into the bedroom and headed for the closet to find all of Denise's belongings gone. He went down the hall to the baby's nursery and everything was gone. Kenneth leaned back up against the wall and slowly slid down until he was in a sitting position will his legs bent. The tears rolled down his face. He didn't know what to do. He was torn between the love of his life and the woman who nursed him back to good health.

Kenneth continued to sit as flashes of Denise and the baby appeared in his head and then he sees Gladys.

"God, what am I to do?"

Kenneth cried out as he looked up, as if he was expecting answers to come flowing down. Then he realized Denise had moved in with Scott. Anger stirred inside of him as he thought about it.

Kenneth got up off the floor, walked into his room, grabbed his belongings and headed out to go back to Gladys.

Kenneth knew he had to have a talk with Scott about the business, but he wanted to get as far away as possible.

Kenneth hopped on the interstate and as he drove, he thought about Gladys and then Denise. He tried to clear his mind and focus on little Kenneth, but he couldn't.

"Why, why did this have to happen to me?"

Kenneth hit his hand against the steering wheel as he was driving.

Two hours later, he pulled into the driveway. He turned off the engine and sat for a while just thinking until he heard a knock at his window. Kenneth looked up to find Gladys standing there.

Kenneth removed the key from the ignition, opened the door and got out.

"How long have you been sitting out here?"

"I don't know. Why?"

"I'm just surprised to see you. I thought you stayed in Indiana"

Kenneth walked past Gladys and into the house. He was feeling a certain way, and he didn't understand why.

Gladys followed Kenneth into the home. She could sense something wasn't right with him.

"Kenneth, are you okay?" Gladys asked.

"I'm good."

Kenneth walked into the kitchen and walked over to the refrigerator, he opened it and grabbed a beer and walked back into the living room and took a seat. Gladys watched Kenneth's every move. She was trying her best to figure out what's up with him when she realized it was Denise.

"Kenneth, are you here for good?"

"I don't know. I have to set up a meeting with my business partner and I guess I will go from there."

"Are you where you want to be?"

"I'm here, aren't I?"

"It appears you're here in spirit, but your mind seems like it's somewhere else."

"Um…"

"Don't do me any favors by staying here with me and it's not where you want to be."

Kenneth stood and walked over to Gladys. He pulled her to him and devoured her mouth. Just then, he realized where he wanted to be. Where he had to be.

Later that night, Kenneth tossed and turned all night. His thoughts were of the love of his life. He dreamed that she had come to him in her birthday suit and they made sweet, passionate love. He awakened from his dream and reached over for Gladys. He climbed between her legs and inserted himself inside of her, and two minutes later; he released himself.

The next morning, the sound of baby Kenneth awakened Denise. She crawled out of bed and made her way over to him. She picked him up and made her way into the kitchen. Denise prepared a bottle of her breast milk for Kenneth. Once she finished, she sat at the kitchen table and fed him. Her thoughts stay on daddy Kenneth and how her heart ached for him.

"God, I wish things were different."

Kenneth sat at the kitchen table, drinking his coffee and watching the morning news. His mind stayed focused on the matter at hand and how bad he felt for what he was about to do to someone's heart. Then his thoughts went to his son, and he smiled. He couldn't believe he had a son, he just wished his mom and dad could see him, but he knew they could see him one day soon.

Gladys walked into the entryway of the kitchen and stood there looking at Kenneth, who looked like his mind was a million miles away.

"Good morning," Gladys said as she walked into the kitchen and interrupted Kenneth's thoughts.

"Good morning."

"What are your plans today?"

"I have to go back to Indy and take care of some loose ends."

"Will I see you later?"

"Why wouldn't you?"

Again, he was going back and forth with his thoughts and decision.

"I didn't know if maybe you've changed your mind about us."

Kenneth didn't respond. He thought about what she just said and how close she was to the truth, but fortunately for her, he had second thoughts about leaving her and the state of Ohio.

Mid-morning, Denise was sitting in the living room watching TV while baby Kenneth slept and while Pebbles got ready for work.

Denise flicked through the channels, trying to find something to watch, something that would occupy her mind and keep her thoughts away from Kenneth.

Pebbles walked into the living room. And she sees Denise looking a little lost right now.

"Hey girl, is everything okay?"

"Yeah, I'm just trying to keep my mind occupied with other thoughts. I need to get back to work".

"No, you need this time to rest and to get your mind right."

"What do you mean get my mind, right?"

"It's obvious to all of us you're not thinking straight. You left a man's home that you're in love with and have a child with because of some things that have happened that was out of his control. He loves you, Denise, and you just left him and let him go to be with another woman. You made his decision too easy."

Denise sat in silence and took in everything that Pebbles had said.

"But Pebbles, you don't understand. What if I had stayed and later he decided that he wanted to be with her and then tried to take Kenneth from me? I couldn't handle that. I would lose my freaking mind."

"Oh my God! Denise, this man put everything on the line for you. He risked his life and his job when he took you out of that apartment. Do you know he could have lost his licenses if Perry would have called the police on him and Scott? He almost died behind that and you're going just up and leave him?"

"Pebbles, do you think Kenneth would really choose me over a white woman?"

"Oh my God! That's what it is. You think because Kenneth is white that he would rather be with his own kind. Girl, you are crazy, Denise, you have his child that's something that no one else has and you said it yourself that he loves black women. Girl, you better wake the hell up and go get your man."

Denise continued to sit. She thought about everything.

"You know what, you are so right. I am going to go and get my man."

Denise got up off the couch and walked over to the TV and cut it off.

Denise pulled up in front of the condo. She sat for a minute before getting out. She looked around for Kenneth's car, but it was nowhere in sight. Denise got out of the car and walked around to the passenger side and to the back door and got Kj out. She made her way up the walkway to the front door and inserted the key into the lock and went inside.

Denise went straight to the living room and sat the baby down on the floor. She went into the bedroom to see if Kenneth had been back.

Once Denise was in the bedroom, she looked around and she could tell Kenneth hadn't slept there. When she went to the closet, Kenneth's clothes are gone. Her heart dropped to her stomach.

"Oh, my god!" Denise cried out, "Why God, why?"

Denise lay there in a fetal position crying until she heard the baby crying. She found the strength to get up off of the floor and made her way back into the living room to Kenneth.

He's gone Kenneth, he left us for another woman.

Denise picked Kenneth up and held him in her arms and began rocking back and forth, looking down at him as the tears fell.

Later that evening, Denise was in the kitchen cooking dinner when Pebbles walked through the door. She let her nose lead her into the kitchen.

"Damn girl, you got it smelling good up in here. What is this you're cooking?"

"Some Steak, fried potatoes with corn and some fried biscuits. Are you hungry?"

"Hell yeah. I ate lunch kind of early today." Pebbles said.

"Well, get your plate."

Pebbles grabbed her a plate from the cabinet and started pulling food on her plate.

"So, was Kenneth there when you got there? Girl, I can't wait to hear what happened."

Pebbles took a seat at the dinner table and waited to hear the news. Denise took a seat and said grace before digging in.

"Girl, if you don't spill it!"

"Girl, if you don't calm the fuck down. He wasn't even there, and it looks like he went back to her."

Pebbles stopped chewing and looked over at Denise in disbelief.

"Please close your mouth before something falls out."

"Denise, how do you know that?"

"His clothes were gone."

CHAPTER ELEVEN

Kenneth went inside the bank and strolled over to the gentlemen sitting behind the desk.

"How can I help you today?" The bank clerk asked.

"I need to get into my safe deposit box."

"I will need to see some ID." The bank clerk said.

The bank clerk verified Kenneth's ID.

"Okay, sir, I'll need your signature right here."

The clerk escorted Kenneth inside the vault

Kenneth pulled out his safe deposit box and grabbed a small black velvet box out. He opened it and admired what was inside and closed the box back and waved over the bank clerk.

"I'm done here."

Kenneth pulled out his cell phone and dialed Scott's number.

"Scott, Kenneth, I'm heading into the office, we need to talk."

"Okay, I'll clear my schedule for two hours."

Kenneth pulled into his parking spot and sat there, glancing around. Nothing had changed, he thought. Kenneth got out and made his way up the walkway to the front door. Kenneth moved over to the set of elevators and pushed the up button and waited for the elevator to arrive. Within seconds, the elevator doors opened.

Kenneth stepped off the elevator and turned left toward his and Scott's law firm. His steps were slow, he seemed like he was walking in slow motion. Filled with unfamiliar emotions, it thrilled him, it angered him and hurt at the same time.

Kenneth stood right outside the office door thinking about how to approach the situation without losing control.

Kenneth walked through the door of the law firm and sees his secretary CeCe.

"Oh, my God! I heard you had resurfaced. I'm just upset that you didn't even bother to come by to see me, Kenneth."

CeCe stood, walked around her desk and walked over to Kenneth and hugged him.

"You don't know how glad I was when I heard the news that you were alive," CeCe said as she took a step back to look at Kenneth and smiled.

"You know Denise works here now as Scott's secretary."

"I heard."

CeCe could sense some tension, "Kenneth, is everything okay?"

"It couldn't be better," Kenneth lied. Just then Scott walked out of his office and greeted Kenneth.

"CeCe, Kenneth and I will be in the conference room so I will need for you to hold all my calls."

"Sure, and it's nice having you back, Kenneth."

Kenneth winked at her and followed Scott into the conference room.

Inside the conference room, both men sat at the table, eyeing each other, not sure how to break the ice when Kenneth spoke.

"You know seeing you at my place the other day shirtless had my mind going a mile a minute. I may have jumped to some conclusions, so I am here now asking you what is going on with you and Denise?"

Scott was truthful with Kenneth, "I will be honest with you. After your disappearance and finding out that Denise was pregnant with your child. I stepped up to the plate like I know you would have wanted me to, but I fell for her, but she wasn't having it so I left that idea alone. And that is the God's honest truth."

"So why were you there with your shirt off?"

Scott laughed and clapped his hands together, "Thanks to your son and my nephew, I was shirtless because I was feeding him and when he finished, I held him over my shoulder to burp him and he spit all of his milk out on me. I took my shirt off so Denise could wash it. But see, you didn't want to listen to anyone, you just jumped to conclusions."

Kenneth had to laugh, "You are right. When I saw you at my front door, I lost all my common sense. I wanted to beat your ass."

"I understand and If it had been the other way around, I would have beat your ass."

Both men laughed.

"So when are you coming back to work?"

"I have a few loose ends to tie up first. I should be back in about two weeks. I want to spend some time with my son and get acquainted with him. One last thing, is Denise staying with you?"

"What? Why would you ask that?"

"She's not at the house anymore."

"That's right, you asked her to leave."

"That was out of anger, but then I came back the next day and told her she could stay."

"I haven't heard from her. She's probably with one of her cousins. Have you checked with Pebbles, Jan or CeCe?"

"No, I just assumed she was staying with you."

"See, there you go assuming. When you assume you make an ass out of yourself."

"I know, I know."

"Now You know you're not leaving out of here without telling me what happened."

Kenneth and Scott sat in the conference room for an hour or more talking, they aired out everything

"Thank you very much for doing what you have done for Denise and my son."

"No problem, I just hope you would have done the same for me."

"And you know it, but I wouldn't have tried to step to your girl though."

"Man, you need to let that go, nothing happened."

Kenneth laughed, "I believe you. I'm just messing with you."

Kenneth walked out of the office feeling much better. He realized what he had to do now.

Kenneth sat in his car thinking, and then he pulled out the velvet box and opened it. He looked at the platinum Cushion Cut Pink Diamond Soleste Engagement Ring he purchased ten months ago. He just hoped she liked it.

He headed back to Cincinnati to see Gladys. He had something to talk to her about.

Hours later, Kenneth pulled into Gladys' driveway. He grabbed the box and slipped it into his pocket and exited the car.

Kenneth came through the door and called out to Gladys, "Gladys, are you up."

"Yes, Kenneth, I'm in here."

Kenneth moved down the hall to the bathroom to find Gladys standing at the sink washing her face. Kenneth pulled her to him.

"Come here, I need to talk to you about something."

Kenneth guided Gladys down the hall to the living room area. He pulled out of his pocket the black box and opened it. Gladys' eyes lit up.

"I purchased this ring ten months ago. This ring was for the woman whom I was in love with, but shit happened. When I got this out of my safe deposit box, the other day and saw how beautiful the ring is, I thought of you. I wanted to give this ring to you, but."

The light slowly went out of Gladys' eyes as she sees Kenneth's expression.

"But what?"

"When I met Denise, I fell in love with her. When I met you, I thought I was in love, but now, I know I loved you because you nursed me back to good health, not that I fell in love with you. I hope that you can understand what I'm saying?"

Gladys took a step back from Kenneth

"You know, I could be angry and upset with you, but I can't. I knew what I was getting myself into when I started falling for you. I knew there was a possibility that you might regain your memory and realize that you have a family. Kenneth, be with the woman and the child you love."

Kenneth pulled Gladys to him and looked down at her.

"Thank you so much for all that you have done for me and for being so understanding."

Kenneth gathered all his belongings at Gladys' and said goodbye

Gladys stood in the doorway and watched as Kenneth left her home and heart.

The next morning, Kenneth awakened in his bed. He scanned the room and remembered where he was. He threw the covers back and threw his legs over the side of the bed, stood and stretched. He made his way to the kitchen for his morning cup of coffee. Kenneth looked in the cabinet where he always kept his coffee to find no coffee. He went to the refrigerator to find it empty.

"Damn!"

Kenneth went back into the bedroom to get dressed to go grocery shopping. Kenneth dressed and stood at the dresser. He grabbed his keys and sees an envelope addressed to him. Kenneth opened the envelope and pulled out the letter.

Kenneth

Just so you know, Denise and the baby will stay with me until you guys get your shit together. I know you still love her and she still loves you so just don't waste too much time figuring that out.

Pebbles

Kenneth smiled as he held the letter to his chest.

"You damn right I do."

Kenneth stood at the door knocking at 8 in the morning.

Pebbles walked to the door and smiled when she sees Kenneth.

"Well, it's about damn time."

Kenneth hugged Pebbles.

"Thank you so much! Where is she?"

Pebbles pointed to the bedroom on the right

Kenneth walked down the hall to the room on the right. He turned the knob slowly and pushed the door open to find Denise and baby Kenneth asleep in the bed. Kenneth walked further into the room and stood over them, smiling.

Denise could feel someone staring at her and opened her eyes to see a tall, handsome white man standing over her. She adjusted her eyes until she recognized who it was.

Denise rose, "Kenneth, what are you doing here and how did you find me?"

"Don't worry about that, just know that I am here for you and my baby."

Kenneth pulled her up into his arms and kissed her.

"I love you, Denise."

Denise pulled back from him and looked at him, "Do you really love me, Kenneth?"

Kenneth pulled out the black box from his jacket, "I bought this for you ten months ago."

Kenneth opened the box and showed Denise, who eyes lit up. Kenneth got down on his knees.

"Denise, I realize now that I cannot live without you and now that we have a son, I want to spend the rest of my life with the two of you, so, Denise, will you marry me?"

Pebbles stood in the hallway looking at the two, "Hell yeah, she will!" Pebbles yelled.

"Yes, I will, Kenneth," Denise said as the tears rolled down her face.

Kenneth grabbed her and kissed her.

CHAPTER TWELVE

Two months later, Denise and her cousins were at David's Bridal trying on wedding and bridesmaid's dresses.

"It looks like we found our dresses," Jan said."

"I think I have found the one," Denise said.

"Girl, you said that about five dresses ago," CeCe yelled.

"I know, but they are all so beautiful, I think I am going with this one here," Denise walked out and the girl's eyes lit up.

"Oh, my God! You look amazing," Pebbles said.

"I feel amazing. I am so excited. I never thought this would happen to me."

"I don't know why not," Jan said.

"I never thought I could be able to get away from Perry let alone find someone who's stable, good looking and loves me for me."

"Girl please, you could have gotten rid of Perry's ass a long time ago. You know damn well we have men in the family that would have taken care of him for you," Pebbles said.

"I know, but I didn't want any of them getting into any trouble behind my decision, but my man loved me enough to get me out the right way and I will always love him for that no matter what happens."

"Enough talking, let's get these dresses sized and paid for so we can eat," CeCe said.

"Hungry ass," Jan said.

The ladies laughed.

"What would I do without you clowns?" Denise asked.

"Denise, you wouldn't know what to do without us," Pebbles said.

"So where are we going to eat?" CeCe asked.

"Let's go to the Outback," Denise said.

"Are you paying?" CeCe asked.

"Why do I have to pay? Your hungry ass is the one who wanted to eat in the first place."

"I got you, cuz," Jan said.

Denise shook her head, "I guess I can pay for lunch since you guys have had my back lately."

Later that evening, Denise was in the kitchen cooking dinner, while Kenneth sat in the living room feeding the baby when they heard a knock at the front door.

"I'll get it," Denise said.

Denise walked to the front door and sees a delivery man.

"Can I help you?"

"Yes, I have a delivery for a Kenneth James."

"Who are these from?" Denise asked.

"Ma'am, read the card."

Just then Kenneth walked up.

"These are for you," Denise said as she handed him the roses for the baby.

Kenneth pulled the card out, opened it and read it.

Kenneth

I just found out today that I am HIV positive, so I suggest you get tested ASAP.

Love Gladys

From the look on his face, Denise could tell something was wrong.

Denise took the card from his hand and read it.

Denise screamed as she let the card fell to the ground.

"Oh my God, Kenneth, how could you put my life in jeopardy?" Denise screamed.

Kenneth moved to comfort her, but she pushed him away.

"Denise, please calm down, we don't even know if this is even true and who says I have contracted the virus? This could be just a ploy to tear us apart. "

Denise paced back and forth with the baby in her arms.

"I knew this was just too damn good to be true."

"What are you talking about?"

"You, me, this right here."

"What are you trying to say, Denise?"

"Nothing good ever happens to me without something bad happening."
Kenneth shook his head.
"Here, take him, I need to get away for a while."
Denise handed the baby to Kenneth.

Twenty minutes later, Denise pulled into Jan's apartment complex.
"Thank God she's home."
Denise got out and walked up the walkway and up the stairs to Jan's apartment. She knocked three times before Jan opened the door.
"Girl, what's wrong?"
Denise broke down crying.
"Denise, what is wrong?"
"Kenneth... he may have HIV."
"What the hell! Where's the baby?"
"Kenneth has him. I needed to get away."
"Come on, let's sit down and talk."
"Where's Ilaya?"
"She's with my friend. Now how do you know Kenneth has HIV?"
"Gladys stupid ass had some roses delivered to him and attached a card saying she just tested positive for it and that he should get tested as soon as possible."
"What! That doesn't even sound right. Why would she wait two months later to get tested? She was probably fucking someone else and got it from him if she even has it. Girl, I wouldn't get all upset about this until you find out if he has it or not."
"I guess you're right. I just lost my mind when I read the card."
"You did exactly what she wanted you to do. Don't you do anything to mess up what you have with Kenneth behind her stupidity."
"Girl, what would I do without your level head? I know Pebbles and CeCe would be ready to whip some ass if I had told them."
"Yeah, you know their crazy asses," Jan said. "You know when you have something good going, the devil will send people to try to

destroy it so don't fall for the bullshit. Just keep your faith, pray and put it in God's hands and don't worry about it."

The following Monday, Kenneth and Denise both got tested, and when they arrived home, they found a letter addressed to Denise from Gladys.

"If I were you, Denise, I wouldn't even read it."

"Yeah, I probably shouldn't read it, but it will worry me all damn day if I don't," Denise said as she made her way inside the house and into the kitchen.

"You know, I still want to be angry with you for getting involved with her."

"Babe, let it go, please."

"I've been praying about it, but it is very hard for a woman to just let it go, knowing her man was in love with another woman. How do you think you would feel if the shoe was on the other foot?"
Denise asked as she moved to stand in front of Kenneth. "Look how you reacted when you thought I was seeing Scott."
Kenneth threw his hands up, "You got a point, there."

"Okay, so don't tell me to just let it go. It's difficult, but I am trying because I want what we have. You have no idea how you make me feel."

"Why don't you tell."
Kenneth said as he pulled Denise to him.

"I can do more than tell you, I can show you, but only after we get our test results back."

"Okay, I can handle that, but I am not worried. I know I am negative."

"Let's just pray that we both are and in the meantime, I will read your bitch's letter."
Kenneth laughed, "You are something else."
After reading the letter, Denise laughed.

"Will she ever stop? Now she's pregnant with your child."
Kenneth laughed, "Even if she is, I will not go back to her and you can believe that."
Denise tossed the letter over by Kenneth.

"Answer this for me and be truthful, how do you feel about her?"

"No, we are not doing this today."

Kenneth walked out of the kitchen with the baby, which infuriated Denise.

"Kenneth, you can't keep avoiding my question. Why is it so hard for you to answer it unless you still love her? Is that it Kenneth?" Denise asked as she walked into the living room.

"Denise, I told you I was not doing this with you, what is your fucking problem?" Kenneth yelled as he stood up.

Denise was speechless. She had never seen Kenneth like this before. His eyes turned a distinct color, which kind of frightened her.

Denise stood there with tears in her eyes.

"You can't leave well enough alone, can you?"

Denise felt hurt. She assumed he still had feelings for Gladys, and this was the reason he wanted to avoid answering her question.

Kenneth couldn't tell Denise how much he missed Gladys and how part of him ached for her, but he wanted to be there with Denise and baby Kenneth and because he truly loved her. He loved Gladys differently.

Denise walked out of the living room and into the bedroom where she broke down. How can I be with a man who's in love with someone else? She said to herself. Denise believed Kenneth was only with her because of the baby.

CHAPTER THIRTEEN

The next couple of days were awkward for them. They found out they were both negative for HIV, which was a relief, but things were still rocky because of what Kenneth had not said.

Kenneth drove to Cincinnati to Mercy hospital to see one nurse name Tequila Sims.

Kenneth pulled into the hospital parking lot and made his way to the elevator. Once he was off the elevator, he made his way to the nurse's station.

One nurse remembered him. "Hey green eyes, how are you?" Nurse Charene Cole, asked.

"I'm good and you?".

"Now that I have seen you, I am much better," the nurse smiled. Kenneth laughed.

"What brings you here?" Charene asked.

"I am here to see Nurse Tequila Sims."

"Okay, at first I thought you were here to see Gladys."

"Oh, no."

"That's good because that lady there is bad news," she said as she walked around the desk to stand in front of Kenneth. "Tequila is on her lunch break, but I know she won't mind you popping in on her. Follow me." Charene escorted Kenneth to the nurse's lunchroom, where he found Tequila Sims eating lunch.

 "Hey Tequila, look who I found."

"Oh my God! How are you?" Tequila asked as she stood up to hug Kenneth.

"I'm good. I came to talk to you about something."

"Okay, pull up a chair. Would you like some lunch?"

"No, I'm good, but thanks."

"So what can I do for you?"

"I need for you to tell me about Gladys." Kenneth told her the situation with Gladys.

Tequila laughed.

66

"Don't you believe that bullshit. That bitch is nothing but a liar. She can't even have kids. She had a hysterectomy some years ago and as far as her being HIV positive, now I don't know about that, but I know she ain't pregnant."

"Well, my fiancee and I got tested and we are both HIV negative."

"Well, I am glad to hear that. You need to stay away from Gladys. I don't know how many marriages she has destroyed. They have even written her up because every attractive man that's admitted to Mercy hospital, she has tried to latch onto. She's a pretty lady, but she's not wrapped too tight up there." Tequila said as she pointed to her head.

"I believe that," Kenneth said.

As weeks went by, Denise started having second thoughts about the wedding. She was in a poor mood, and she didn't want to do anything or be around anyone. She was slowly falling into a state of depression and no one could get her out of it. Kenneth called her cousins, thinking they could help.

Her cousin tried their best to get her out of the house, but they were unsuccessful.

"Denise, snap the hell out of this mood, girl," Jan said.

"I know you are wrecking my fucking nerves," Pebbles said as she walked over to look out the window.

"Y'all leave my cousin alone. She's going through something right now and we need to be by her side and have some compassion," CeCe said as she moved to sit down on the bed where Denise was sitting.

"Damn, how much compassion are we supposed to have?" Pebbles asked.

"You are so cold-hearted. You better hope you never have to go through something like this," CeCe said.

"I guess we were a little harsh," Jan said.

"You think?" CeCe said sarcastically.

Pebbles walked over to the bed, took her shoes off and crawled into bed with her cousin and Jan followed. The four of them sat on the bed with Denise while CeCe wrapped her arms around her.

"We are here sweetheart and we will always have your back," CeCe said.

Denise looked up at CeCe with tears in her eyes, "thank you, cuz."

A week later, Kenneth got home from work to find no dinner, the baby crying and Denise in bed. Kenneth walked over to pick the baby up, changed his diaper and fed him. He was so pissed that his son was wringing wet.

"Denise, we need to talk," Kenneth said as he walked back into the bedroom.

"Something has got to change around here."

Denise raised up, "Or what, you will run back to Gladys. That's where you want to be anyway, so why don't you carry your ass back to her."

Just then, it dawned on Kenneth what had caused the turnabout in Denise's attitude.

"So all of this is about Gladys? Are you kidding me?"

Denise got up and walked out of the room into the bathroom where she slammed the door shut.

When she reopened the door, Kenneth was standing right there.

"We will deal with this shit right now."

Kenneth guided Denise to the bed, and they both took a seat.

"I love you woman, what else do I have to do? If I wanted Gladys, I would be there with her. If things don't work out between us, I will not be with Gladys. I do still love Gladys, but not in the way you think. I love her because she took me in when I had no one and nowhere else to go. Every day while I was in a coma, she would come and talk to me as often as she could. She nursed me back to where I am today and for that, I love her and to be honest, I miss her. I miss her silly sense of humor and the fact that she was so understanding and so kind."

Denise looked over at Kenneth, "Really, is that why the bitch lied and said she was HIV positive and that she was pregnant. Is that the type of woman you love?"

"I don't know who that woman is. That is not the same woman who helped me."

"Um…"

"Can we get things back to the way they used to be?"

"There are some things that I will have to work out within myself and once I am together, I think we can do that."

Kenneth moved over and pulled Denise to him, "I love you more than life."

Kenneth kissed Denise and laid her down, "Now, can I have some of this," Kenneth asked as he moved his hand down between her legs.

"Why don't you join me in the shower."

"Well, all right then."

Denise slowly let go of the anger that she carried about Kenneth and Gladys. She started hanging out with her cousins again and they planned the wedding, which was in three months.

"What can we cross off our to-do list?" Denise asked.

"We have our dresses, the church and the hall for the reception. We have the caterer and the DJ booked. We need decorations for the church and the hall." Jan said.

"What about the honeymoon," Pebbles asked. That's the second most important thing."

"I got that handled," Denise said.

"So where are you guys going?" CeCe asked.

"We are spending four days in London and four days in Paris."

"All right now," Jan said.

"You know I have always wanted to go to Paris and Kenneth wants to go to London so we are going to both places."

"Shit, that ass will come home pregnant," Pebbles said.

They all burst out laughing.

"Naw, I don't think so. I love my man, but I am not trying to have a house full of kids. I have dreams and goals and with a bunch of kids, it will put my dreams on hold."

"You are right. What do you want to do?"

"Okay, but don't laugh. I have always wanted to be a filmmaker."

"So what's funny about that?" Jan asked.

69

"Nothing, but you know how some people are. They have no dreams or ambitions, and when they see people who do, they always have something negative to say about it."

"I think that's great," Pebbles said.

"Me too," CeCe chimed in.

"Well, I am glad you guys understand."

"Have you found a school to attend?" Jan asked.

"No, but Kenneth said, if I can't find a school here in Indy, he will hire a local filmmaker to teach me. My man is so damn good to me."

"Yes, he is." Pebbles agreed.

"Oh, my God! I forgot all about the invitations." Denise said.

"I will put it on the list," Jan said.

"Do you want a certain color?" CeCe asked.

"Girl, I haven't even thought about it. I guess white will do."

"White or cream?" Pebbles asked.

"Um… let's go with cream. Oh, I forgot to tell you girls, Kenneth has a couple of single brothers and cousins who also like black women."

"All silky silky now," CeCe said.

"Look, my little man is awake. He is so good, he just lays there until mommy comes and gets him." Denise said as she picked him up.

"Let me hold him," CeCe held her arms out for him.

"Here, let me warm up his milk."

"Do you still breastfeed him?"

"Yes, but I am trying to get him to nurse from a bottle. I'm so tired of men sucking on my tits. If it ain't his daddy, it's him."

"You are so silly,' Pebbles said.

"Well, at least you have someone to suck on them?" Jan said.

Denise walked back into the room, "Do you want me to feed him or do you want to?"

Just then there was a knock at the front door.

"You can do it," CeCe said. CeCe hands Kj to Denise.

"Jan, can you get the front door for me?"

Jan walked to the front door and yelled to Denise, "Girl, there's a white woman knocking at your door."

"What! Here hold him," Denise said as she handed Kj to CeCe.

70

Pebbles followed Denise to the front door.

"What is this bitch doing here?" Denise asked.

"Who is she?" Pebbles asked.

"The is the bitch Kenneth was with in Cincinnati."

"Oh, no, she didn't. Let me handle this bitch," Pebbles said.

"No, Pebbles, we don't need you getting yourself in trouble on my account. I will handle this bitch."

Denise unlocked the front screen and opened the door.

"Gladys, what the hell do you want?"

"Is Kenneth here?" Gladys said with an attitude.

"This bitch has the nerve to have an attitude," Jan said.

By this time, CeCe walked in with the baby, "Cuz, do you need me to handle this?"

"No, CeCe."

"Gladys, Kenneth is not here, and if he was your ass wouldn't be seeing him so take your lying ass home."

"Lying ass?" Gladys asked.

"Yes, bitch, you pretended to be pregnant by Kenneth and that you had contracted HIV, but we found out that you just lied. Didn't your co-worker Tequila tell you she told Kenneth that you were just lying and was trying to break us up? THOT go home because it ain't going to work," Denise said as she slammed the door in Gladys' face.

"Girl, let me at her," CeCe said.

"She is not worth the energy."

CHAPTER FOURTEEN

Two hours later, Kenneth arrived home. Denise had the entire home smelling good.

"Now, that's my baby," Kenneth said as he walked over to Denise and hugged her.

"Hey babe, I hope you don't mind my cousins having dinner with us?"

"Now, why would I mind? They are family now."

Kenneth walked into the family room and sees the ladies with his baby boy.

"What's up, ladies?"

"Hey, Kenneth."

"CeCe, why weren't you at work today?"

"Kenneth, I told you I was taking a vacation day today and if you didn't know that, why didn't you call me?"

"I did, you didn't answer."

"Oh, sorry," CeCe said after looking at her phone and sees two missed calls from Kenneth.

An hour later, the gang sat around the table feeding their faces.

"You know I am a little afraid to ask this, but what did you ladies do today?" Kenneth asked as he bit into a delicious homemade dinner roll.

"Now why in the hell would you be afraid to ask us what we did?" Pebbles spoke up.

Kenneth laughed, "Because I know how you ladies are sometimes. Trouble, nothing but trouble."

"Oh, I can not believe you," CeCe said.

"Me either," Jan chimed in.."

"Oh, my God! I almost forgot. That crazy bitch of yours came by here today looking for you."

"Who?"

"You know who I'm talking about?"

"Babe, why didn't you call me?"

"Call you for what?"

"We handled the situation," Pebbles said.

"And how did you guys handle it?"

"I told her we knew she lied about everything and I also told her that if you were here, she wouldn't be seeing you and I slammed the door in her face."

"That's good, but the next time she comes, call me. We may have to get a restraining order against her."

That night, Kenneth and Denise lay in bed talking. "I think things will be okay with us," Denise said as she climbed on top of Kenneth.

"You think," Kenneth asked as he kissed Denise on the lips.

"Yes," Denise said as she made her way down his body.

"Make me a believer," Kenneth said.

"I plan to do just that."

Three weeks later, the girls were out shopping as usual. Little Kj was sitting in his car seat watching as the women tried on shoe after shoe.

"I think those shoes there will match your dresses better than the other three," Denise said.

The ladies were busy trying on shoes when Denise looked over at the baby.

"Where's my baby?" Denise asked. "Jan, do you have my baby?"

"No, I thought CeCe had him," Jan said.

"No, he was sitting in his car seat that last time I checked," CeCe said.

"Where is Pebbles? Maybe she has him," Denise said.

Two minutes later, Pebbles returned.

"Pebbles do you have the baby?" CeCe asked.

"No, what's wrong?" Pebbles asked.

"Oh my God! Where's my baby," Denise panicked.

The ladies ran around the store searching for Kj.

"Ms. Have you saw my baby?" Denise asked the sales associate. Just then another sales associate walked up, "What's the problem?"

"My baby is missing!" Denise yelled.

"Did you see anyone walk out of here with a baby," Jan started asking the customers.

"I saw a white lady with blonde hair walk out of her with a mixed baby," one customer said.

Did he have a blue blanket over him?" Denise asked as she made her way over to the lady.

"Yes, he did."

It took the police five minutes to get to the store. In the meantime, Denise phoned Kenneth.

When Kenneth arrived, he was frantic, "What the hell happened?" He asked Denise, who was crying.

"Some white lady walked out of the store with our baby."

"White lady?" Kenneth asked, "Was it Gladys?" Kenneth asked.

"Oh, my God! I didn't think about it being her."

Kenneth pulled out his cell phone and called Gladys. Gladys picked up on the fourth ring She said nothing, and Kenneth didn't need her to say anything because of what he heard in the background. He heard his son crying in the background.

"Kenneth, I want you to come to my home alone, if I even hear a police siren, you will no longer have a son," Gladys said before disconnecting the call.

Kenneth grabbed a hold of Denise and moved her to the other side of the room.

"Gladys has the baby. She wants me to come alone. She said if we call the police, we won't have a son."

"Let's go so I can kick that bitch's ass." Denise was ready to go.

"Denise, did you not hear what I said?"

"That's my baby, I have to go with you," Denise cried.

"Denise, I won't let her hurt him, I promise, but I need to leave without you and without the police knowing about this. I can't take any chances."

"Kenneth, please let me go with you. I promise to stay in the car. She won't see me. I just want to be close by, please," Denise pleaded."

"Denise, I have to get our son. I promise I will bring him back safe and sound."

Denise continued to hold Kenneth tight as the tears continued to pour out.

"Okay, bring my baby back," Denise said before kissing him, "And Kenneth, be careful."

Denise watched as Kenneth walked out. She turned to find her cousins there.

"Gladys has the baby," Denise whispered to her cousins.

"What the fuck," Pebbles yelled.

"Kenneth called her and heard the baby crying in the background. He's on his way there. I'm so afraid for him and the baby."

"Girl, you need to tell the police," Jan said.

"She said she will kill the baby if the police show up."

"Denise, tell the police. They know how to handle situations like this." CeCe said.

Denise thought about what her cousins said, she thought about what Kenneth said.

Denise walked over to the police and told them about Gladys.

"Ma'am, do you have her address?" Officer Wilson Murkison asked.

"No, the only thing I know is that she lives in Cincinnati and works at Mercy Hospital. She said she will kill my baby if the police get involved."

"Okay, just sit tight, I will be right back."

Officer Murkison walked over to his partners to discuss the situation.

"Hey guys, I have more information," the officer said as he filled his partners in on what's going on.

"Man, I have to do something," Denise said as she paced back and forth. "I can't believe I was so stupid not to find out where this bitch lives."

75

Just then, she realized that the flower store must have her home address from when she had those flowers delivered to their home. Denise rushed over to where the officers were standing.

"Excuse me, but I just thought of something. The lady that took my son had some roses delivered to my home. Do you think you can have the store give you her home address?"

"What was the name of the store?" Officer Murkison asked.

"It's called Eagledale Florist."

"Thanks," The officer said.

Officer Murkison walked outside and called the dispatcher and had him contact the store to see if they can find out the address for a Gladys Stone.

Denise and her cousins followed behind the officers. About five minutes later, the dispatcher gave them the address to a Gladys Stone in Cincinnati.

"Write that down," Denise told Jan. "Come on let's go."

"Where are we going?" Jan asked.

"We are going to Cincinnati."

Denise and her cousins hopped in her car and head for Cincinnati.

"Put the address in your GPS," Denise told Pebbles, who was sitting in the front seat.

"See, I should have beat that bitch's ass when she came to the house. I guarantee you she wouldn't have taken the baby, that bitch would have been too scared," CeCe said from the back seat.

"I want y'all to know that if she has hurt my baby, I will probably go to jail because I will kill that lady with my bare hands."

"Well, we will be go to jail right along with you for helping you kill that bitch," Pebbles said.

Three hours later, Denise turned the corner onto Gladys's street. The two police officers greeted her.

They instructed Denise to roll down the window, "Ma'am, we are asking everyone to stay clear of this area right now."

"But I live right there," Denise lied as she pointed to the house next to Gladys.

"I'm sorry ma'am, but I can't let you through."

"Are you serious?" Pebbles asked.

The officer threw his hands up.

Denise backed up and drove around to the next street. She parked in front of a vacant house and cut the engine, "Come on girls, let's do what we have to do," Denise said as she unbuckled her seat belt.

The ladies exited the car and were now standing in front of a vacant home.

"So what are we going to do now?" Jan asked.

"Let's cut through this yard that will lead us to the alley and in back of Gladys's house," Denise said as she took off walking.

They cut through the yard and made their way to the alley and in the back of Gladys's house.

"I'm not trying to climb no fence," Jan said.

"Girl, just open the damn gate," Denise said in frustration.

Pebbles and CeCe laughed as they shook their head.

Denise eased up to the back window of the house and tried to open it, but it was locked.

The ladies stayed behind and watched.

"Damn," Denise said as she continued to pry the window open. Denise looked back and sees that her cousin's had not moved an inch. She motioned for them to come on.

"You guys will get us caught just standing there looking like deer caught in headlights."

The women didn't know what to do, "well, hell, it ain't like we've done this before," Pebbles said.

"Well, hell, I know you have seen this in movies before, just pretend you're in a movie, how hard can that be?"

The three cousins lined themselves up against the house with their back against it. Denise looked back at them and shook her head, "I should have come by myself," she said under her breath.

Denise moved to the edge of the home and peeked around the corner. She stopped in her tracks when she sees a police officer standing on the side of the house. She motioned for the ladies to stay put, "stay here and let me go on the other side to see if there are any windows. Whatever you do, do not move, there's an officer on the side of the house."

Denise made her way around to the other side of the house where she sees another window. She can't get it opened either, but she can see inside of the room. She looked around, and she sees her baby lying in the bed sleep.

"Oh my God!"

CHAPTER FIFTEEN

Inside the house, Kenneth pleaded with Gladys, "please don't hurt my son, he is innocent in all of this."

"Kenneth, we could have been happy together, we were happy until you got your memory back. You know, I don't understand why you would have a baby with that black bitch!"

"See, that's why I could never be with you, you're nothing more than a racist."

"What do you mean you can't be with someone like me? Why are you here? I thought you wanted to be with me?"

"I am here because of my son."

"If I can't have you, Kenneth, Denise will not want you when she learns that you're the reason I killed her son."

"No, Gladys, don't. I will do whatever it is you want me to do," Kenneth pleaded.

Denise could not get the bedroom window opened, so she moved to the next window where she sees Kenneth and Gladys. She stood back, so they could not see her, but continued to listen to their conversation.

"I want us to be together and raise little Kenneth," Gladys said.

"Okay, okay, we can do that."

The more Denise heard, the angrier she got.

"Like hell, you will," Denise said.

"But what about Denise? How can I do that to her?"

"Fuck that bitch, let her find some other man to have a baby with. You know that's all they do anyway is have babies by different men." Kenneth Shook his head.

"I would have never guessed you would have turned out to be the person you are. I see why no one at work likes you."

"They don't like me because they are all jealous of me."

Just then, Kenneth sees a shadow that moved outside the window. Gladys noticed him looking at something and walked over by the window.

"Did you bring someone with you?"

"No, why would I do that?"

"I told you what would happen if you told the police."

Kenneth moved to where Gladys stood and pulled her close to him.

"Why would I do that?" Kenneth asked as he pulled her away from the window.

"Can I go see my son?"

"Sure, come on," Gladys said as she guided Kenneth down the hallway to the second bedroom.

"See, he's resting."

Kenneth walked over to his son, picked him up and kissed him softly on his cheek. Then he turned to Gladys, "why are you doing this, Gladys? You know this will not turn out the way you want it to. I will never love you the way you want me to."

Gladys walked over to the dresser drawer, opened it and removed a gun and pointed it at Kenneth.

"Oh, it will end the way I want it to or you and your son will die!"

"You won't shoot me, you love me," Kenneth said as he moved with his son in his arm and head for the door.

"Don't you dare leave this room! Kenneth, I am not playing with you!"

Denise moved back to the bedroom window and sees Kenneth with the baby in his arms, leaving the room when she sees Gladys pointed the gun and fired one shot, hitting Kenneth in the back. As he went down, Gladys dropped the gun and grabbed the baby and ran out of the room with him.

"Oh, hell naw!" Denise yelled as she took off one of her shoes and slammed it into the window causing the glass to shatter everywhere.

Gladys ran into the bathroom and lay the baby on the floor. She walked over to the bathtub, turned the water on and lays the baby in the tub.

The water slowly filled up while Gladys stood there smiling.

"Drown, you fucking bastard!"

Denise called out for help. "Help me someone, help me," she yelled as she tried to climb through the window.

The three cousins come to her rescue. "Help me reach the window so I can climb through."

"Here, let's put our hands together. Denise step into our hands and we will push you up," CeCe said.

Denise did what they said, and she was halfway through when Kenneth came too.

"Kenneth, Kenneth," Denise called out to him. Kenneth looked up to see Denise climbing through the window. He tried to get up and grabbed the gun.

"Where is she?" Denise asked, walking over to him.

The water in the bathtub almost covered baby Kenneth's body and at any minute, the baby would be under water.

Gladys moved closer to the tub and kneed down. She placed her hand over the baby's face and pushed down.

"Kenneth, where is she?" Denise asked.

"I don't know." Kenneth barely able to speak.

"Stay here, I will be right back."

Denise moved down the hall where she heard water running. Denise continued to move closer to the sound of the water when she heard water splashing.

"Die, you bastard," Gladys said as the baby moved and splashed water.

Denise ran into the bathroom to find Gladys kneeling over the tub. She moved further into the room to find her baby in the tub fighting for his life.

Denise hit Gladys in the back of the head with the gun, knocking her out. She reached over Gladys and pulled her baby out of the water.

Denise grabbed the baby who was not breathing and ran to the front of the house as the police were kicking down the door down.

"He's not breathing," Denise cried as she ran with the baby to one of the police officers.

"Give him here," One of the police officers said as he performed CPR on the infant.

Kenneth made his way into the living room where he collapsed.

CHAPTER SIXTEEN

Three hours later, Denise and her cousins sat in the waiting area at Mercy Hospital waiting for the doctor to come out and talk with them.

"I have some great news for you ladies," the doctor said. "Daddy and baby are fine, but I want to keep them overnight for observations." Kenneth was lucky. The bullet missed his spine by an inch. He should be able to go home in a couple of days.

"Thank God!" Denise said out loud. "Thank you so much."

Three months later, Kenneth and Denise tied the knot and right after, they were on their way to Paris. They will have a reception and celebration with family and friends when they returned. Kenneth parents offered to babysit their grandchild while they were away.

In Paris

"Oh, my God! This place is outstanding." Denise said as she stood outside on the balcony of their hotel. "Man, if it wasn't for my baby, I would not return to the state."

"Hey, what about your husband?"

"My hubby is here with me already," Denise said as she moved to stand in front of Kenneth. Denise looked up at him, stood on her tippy toes and brushed her lips up against his. "Take me to bed, baby, and love me like you've never loved anyone before."

"Say no more!" Kenneth said.

Kenneth picked his wife up and moved into the room. He stood her on her feet and undressed her until she was in her birthday suit. He then laid her softly down on the bed. He stood above her and removed his clothes slowly, removing one item at a time, giving her an eye full of himself.

"Do you like what you see?" He asked her.

"Yes daddy, I like it a lot."

"Then why don't you show daddy how much you like it."

Denise moved off the bed to stand in front of Kenneth. She kneeled down before him. She moved closer to his body and licked Kenneth's balls, one ball at a time. She then moved to his penis and ran her tongue around the head several times before taking him into her mouth.

Back in the states

Denise's cousins were so angry about what Gladys tried to do to their baby cousin that she got herself arrested along with her sister to be in jail with Gladys .

As they entered the lockup holding cell, they saw Gladys sitting there talking with some other inmates on the other side of the floor. Renee and Tess sat down on the other side of the wall on the bench, eyeing her. Gladys and the other ladies looked over at them and one inmate asked, "Do you guys have a fucking problem?"

Renee and Tess looked at each other and laughed.

"Yeah, we got a problem, but not with you, but if you want to be a problem too, we will allow that." Renee and Tess stood up.

"Naw, we cool," the big mouth lady said.

Later that evening in their cell, they watched as the guard walked Gladys down to her cell.

Renee and Tess's cousin, the guard, passed Renee a shank and said, "You have one chance to take care of her before they move her tomorrow morning."

"Gotcha," Renee said.

Gladys's cell

Renee and Tess left their cell as their cousin stood guard and walked down to Gladys cell and stood there looking at her.

"What the fuck do you want?" Gladys asked.

"I'm so glad you asked that question," Tess said.

"Do you know my cousin Denise and Kenneth James? Remember what you tried to do to my little cousin, Kj?" Tess said as she moved further into the room.

Renee stood outside the cell keeping a lookout.

"Well, I'm here to do to you what you tried to do to little Kj, bitch!"

Renee grabbed Gladys and throw her on the ground. She pulled her by her leg over to the toilet and grabbed her up and stuck her head down the toilet. Gladys tried to break loose but she couldn't Gladys struggled for about three minutes before she gave up.

Tess grabbed Gladys by the hair and throw her on the floor. She stood up and walked over to her, bent down and slit her throat. Tess put the shank into Gladys's hand to make it look like a suicide.

Renee and Tess slowly walked back to their cell and winked at the guard
.

The next morning the guards found Gladys dead in her cell, but the police believed they murdered her.

The End

The author
Denise Hill

www.ingramcontent.com/pod-product-compliance
Lightning Source LLC
Chambersburg PA
CBHW080835250626
47160CB00008B/2947